Skating

Blue Skate Dreams

School

Linda Chapman

Illustrated by Nellie Ryan

PUFFIN

Madame Letsworth's Magic Ice-Skating Academy

FROST FAIRIES

MOLLY HANNAH EMILY TILDA ALICE

ICE OWLS

AMANDA ZOE HEATHER TASHA OLIVIA

SNOW FOXES

CAMILLA TESS CLARE HELENA

To my wonderful Amany — the huskies are for you!

PUFFIN BOOKS

Published by the Penguin Group
Penguin Books Ltd, 80 Strand, London WC2R 0RL, England
Penguin Group (USA) Inc., 375 Hudson Street, New York, New York 10014, USA
Penguin Group (Canada), 90 Eglinton Avenue East, Suite 700, Toronto, Ontario, Canada M4P 2Y3
(a division of Pearson Penguin Canada Inc.)
Penguin Ireland, 25 St Stephen's Green, Dublin 2, Ireland (a division of Penguin Books Ltd)
Penguin Group (Australia), 250 Camberwell Road, Camberwell, Victoria 3124, Australia
(a division of Pearson Australia Group Pty Ltd)
Penguin Books India Pvt Ltd, 11 Community Centre, Panchsheel Park, New Delhi – 110 017, India
Penguin Group (NZ), 67 Apollo Drive, Rosedale, North Shore 0632, New Zealand
(a division of Pearson New Zealand Ltd)
Penguin Books (South Africa) (Pty) Ltd, 24 Sturdee Avenue, Rosebank, Johannesburg 2196, South Africa

Penguin Books Ltd, Registered Offices: 80 Strand, London WC2R 0RL, England

puffinbooks.com

First published 2010
1

Text copyright © Linda Chapman, 2010
Illustrations copyright © Nellie Ryan, 2010
All rights reserved

The moral right of the author and illustrator has been asserted

Set in 15/22 pt Bembo
Typeset by Palimpsest Book Production Limited, Grangemouth, Stirlingshire
Made and printed in England by Clays Ltd, St Ives plc

British Library Cataloguing in Publication Data
A CIP catalogue record for this book is available from the British Library

ISBN: 978-0-141-32637-5

www.greenpenguin.co.uk

Penguin Books is committed to a sustainable future
for our business, our readers and our planet.
The book in your hands is made from paper
certified by the Forest Stewardship Council.

Contents

In the Magic Land of Ice and Winter . . .

Everything looked just as it always did.
A blanket of snow covered the fields
and meadows, towns and villages.
Frozen lakes glittered in the rays of the
pale sun and a mist hung over the tops
of the jagged mountains. Silvery robins
darted from tree to tree while white
fluffy fox cubs tumbled after each other.
But the ice sylphs who lived in the land

knew something was different.

At the edge of the land, one of the mountains had changed shape. Something had curled around it, great wings folded flat. Its dark-red scaly sides moved in and out and great jets of fire streamed out of its mouth. Around the vast creature all the frozen rivers had melted and the branches of the trees had started to sprout green leaves. Every so often an avalanche of softened snow would hurtle down the mountainside, picking up stones and rocks and sweeping away everything in its path with a loud roar.

The headteacher of the Magic Ice-skating Academy, Madame Letsworth, frowned thoughtfully as she watched the fourteen human girls skating on the ice rink. In two weeks, one of them would be chosen to be the Ice Princess, a girl who would have the power to save this magic land.

Madame Letsworth's eyes flicked from one pupil to another. None of them knew yet what the Ice Princess would have to do or how she would be chosen. What would they say when they found out?

Chapter One
Husky Driving

Emily and her two best friends, Hannah and Molly, stood in the snow with the other girls from the Academy. 'Look how fast they're going!' gasped Emily as four tall ice sylphs each expertly drove a team of barking huskies in and out of a line of pine trees. All the ice sylphs who lived in the Land of Ice and Winter had large pointed ears, but otherwise they looked just like humans.

'I want to have a go!' said Molly eagerly.

'It looks quite tricky,' commented Hannah, nervously twisting her long blonde ponytail.

'It looks amazing!' Emily breathed, watching as rainbow-coloured sparks flew up from under the dogs' claws. She loved all the silver-coated huskies that lived in the kennels in the school grounds – in fact, she loved everything about being at boarding school in the Land of Ice and Winter. All the girls got to spend hours every day ice-skating, and if they weren't skating, they were doing something fun like gymnastics or cross-country skiing or one of Emily's favourite lessons – learning about the amazing land and the magical creatures that lived in it.

That day, the girls were having a new type of lesson because their headteacher, Madame Letsworth, had announced that they were going to learn how to drive husky sledges. There were no roads in the Land of Ice and Winter and the ice sylphs got around the land by skiing, skating or sledging.

Emily could still hardly believe that she was living in this land. She and the other girls had all been magically whisked away from the human world. They had been told they could choose to stay at the school for six weeks and, through magic, no one at home would realize they were gone. At the end of their time there, one of the girls would be chosen to be the Ice Princess. She would perform a task that would help the ice sylphs in some way and, if she was successful, she would be granted a wish. Emily longed to be the Ice Princess!

In two weeks we'll find out which of us it's going to be, she thought excitedly.

'Here they come!' cried Molly as the dogs raced towards them.

'Whoa there!' the husky handlers shouted. The huskies slowed down and came to a stop by the watching girls. The dogs looked round, their tongues hanging out as if they were laughing.

'So, who wants a go?' called Trakin, the head dog handler. He was a rugged ice sylph with blond hair and a beard. Most of the girls put their hands up.

'Let's have Emily, Alice, Tilda and Zoe first,' Trakin called.

'Ohhh,' complained Molly.

Trakin smiled. 'Don't worry. You'll all get a turn in the end.' He pointed each of the girls towards one of the sylphs. Emily was to be with Trakin himself. She tucked her brown shoulder-length hair into her blue woolly hat and walked over to his sledge, her stomach turning double flips in excitement.

She patted the lead dog, a massive husky with a white chest called Ash, and listened carefully as Trakin explained about controlling the dogs and showed her where to stand. Each sledge had runners that were really only big enough for one person to stand on.

Trakin strode behind Emily as she
stood with, one foot on each of the
runners. He showed her how to hold the
reins, one in each hand. 'You bring the
reins down on their backs when you
want them to go forward, and say
"Mush!"' he explained. 'Then, when you
want them to slow down, you say
"Whoa". To turn, you bring both reins
over to the side. We'll start off slowly.
Have you got the reins?' Emily nodded.
'Then off we go!'

Emily gently brought the reins down

on the dogs' backs. They bounced
forward, jerking the sledge underneath
her. If her balance hadn't been so good,
Emily would have toppled off, but she
quickly regained her footing. Trakin was
a good instructor and soon she was
stopping, starting and turning with ease.
The huskies went faster. It was a fantastic
feeling to be pulled through the snow
with the wind whipping against her
cheeks. She drove the sledge in between
the trees and raced back to the waiting
girls.

'That was a very good first attempt,'
Trakin said when it was time to swap
over.

'I loved it!' Emily went to pat all of the
huskies. 'Thank you!' she told them, her
cheeks glowing. 'You were brilliant!'

They crowded round her, licking at her hands and pushing their heads against her legs and arms.

Emily rejoined Molly as Hannah was called to have a turn.

'What was it like?' asked Molly.

'Cool! I want to do it all over again!' Emily declared.

Heather, who was in a different dorm from them, was standing nearby. 'It looks really scary,' she said nervously. She was one of the shyest girls at the Academy. Heather had dark shoulder-length hair and she was in Emily's skating group. 'I'm really worried I won't be able to stop the dogs,' she went on anxiously. 'What if they run off or crash into a tree?'

'You'll be OK,' Emily reassured her.

'You'll have Trakin or one of the other sylphs with you.'

'And the dogs won't crash into a tree. Didn't you know they have extrasensory magical whiskers to stop them from doing that?' Molly said.

Emily frowned. She'd never heard of the huskies having magical whiskers. 'What are you talking about, Molly?'

Molly shot her a look, her dark-brown

eyes twinkling. 'They have,' she said earnestly.

'No!' said Heather. 'Are you sure?'

'Oh, yes,' declared Molly. 'I can't believe you haven't heard about it. Every time they get too near a tree, their whiskers buzz and they know not to go any closer.'

'Wow!' said Heather, wide-eyed. 'That's amazing!'

A giggle rose inside Emily. She knew now that Molly was just teasing. Molly loved playing tricks on people!

'It's true. After all, they're not crashing into any trees now, are they?' Molly said. 'You should tell Trakin how cool you think it is, Heather.'

'I will,' Heather agreed.

Emily burst out laughing. 'You mustn't

tell Trakin, Heather! Molly's just winding
you up.'

Molly giggled. Heather's mouth
dropped open and then she started to
grin. She was easy to trick, but she was
also very good at seeing the funny side. 'I
can't believe I fell for that! Oh, Molly!'
She threw a snowball at Molly.

Molly ducked. 'Just check out those
whiskers!' she grinned as Heather was
called to have her turn. 'Go on, see if
you can feel them buzzing!'

Trakin shot Molly a very puzzled look,
which made Emily giggle even more.

They all had several turns at husky
driving. Some of them, like Emily, took
to it very easily. Others, like Molly, let
the huskies go too fast and almost tipped

their sledge over. Hannah was cautious, but managed the dogs well. Heather was very nervous and not very strong. A couple of times, Trakin had to help her stop the dogs from charging off the way they wanted to go.

'That was brilliant!' Emily said happily after they had finished the lesson by learning how to harness and unharness the patient huskies.

'It was really fun,' agreed Molly as they began to walk back towards the school. She gave a little skip. 'And now there's something even better. We get to find out about this week's competition, remember?'

Every week at the school, the girls took part in a competition for a pair of different coloured skates. In the first week, the competition had been to skate a routine showing that you were dancing with your heart. Emily had won that competition even though she was the least experienced skater in the school. She had been presented with a pair of snow-white skates.

The second week's task had been to skate in pairs and tell a story, which Zoe and Heather had won. The third week had been a two-day scavenger hunt out in the land in teams. Emily, Hannah and Molly had been the winners that time. The fourth week, the girls had had to choreograph their own routine with set moves, and Hannah had won that competition.

And this week, the fifth week . . . Well, they were about to find out. Before they had come out husky driving, Madame Letsworth had told them that she would announce the competition after their lesson.

Emily hurried towards the school with the others. She couldn't wait to find out what Madame Letsworth was going to say!

Chapter Two
Competition News

Ten minutes later, the girls sat in the common room staring at Madame Letsworth.

'We have to drive the huskies in a race?' Molly burst out. 'And ski and skate as well? Brilliant!'

'So we're not skating in the rink?' said Amanda, a pretty girl with long dark hair.

Madame Letsworth shook her head.
'No. This week the competition will be
a relay race. You will be in teams of
three. The first person must drive the
huskies through the forest at the front of
the school and then pass the baton on to
the second team member. That person
will ski across the field to where the third
girl is waiting on the river with her
skates on, and she will race back to the
school. The first team home wins.'

Cool! thought Emily. It sounded like

one of the most exciting competitions they'd been set so far!

'Each member of the winning team will be given a pair of sky-blue skates,' continued Madame Letsworth. 'You can choose your own teams and it will be up to you to decide who will do what. Because there are only fourteen of you, one team will only have two people and so one girl will have to do the skating and the husky driving.'

Amanda groaned. 'Do we *have* to do this?' She hated outdoor activities.

'Yes, Amanda,' Madame Letsworth said firmly.

'But why can't it just be an ice-skating competition?' complained Amanda.

'And why does she always have to whinge so much?' Molly muttered to Emily.

Emily grinned as Madame Letsworth replied to Amanda's question. 'Because the competitions are carefully picked to help us choose who will be our Ice Princess, Amanda. There are fewer than two weeks to go until we make that decision and we need you all to compete. Now, why don't you get into teams?'

Emily, Hannah and Molly quickly grabbed hands. Heather joined up with

Olivia from her dorm as the others formed their own groups. Soon Amanda was the only one left on her own. Emily saw her look round. The choice was between two pairs. There was Camilla and Tess from the Snow Foxes dorm or Heather and Olivia from the Ice Owls, Amanda's own dorm.

Camilla gave her a look as if to say *Don't even think about it*, so Amanda went over to Olivia and Heather instead. Olivia didn't look hugely pleased, but Heather smiled at Amanda in welcome.

'This is going to be really fun!' Molly said to Hannah and Emily. 'Who's going to do what?' But before they had a chance to discuss it, Madame Letsworth had called for silence again.

'Before I leave you, I would like to

tell you a little more about the Ice Princess.'

Silence fell immediately and all the girls looked at their headteacher expectantly. They hadn't been told anything more about the Ice Princess since the day they had first arrived at skating school. They still didn't even know what she would have to do or how exactly she would be chosen, although they'd all been doing a lot of guessing!

Madame Letsworth looked round at them all. 'I told you when you first arrived that the Ice Princess will help us with a problem. And now I am going to tell you a little more about this problem. You have all heard of the fire dragons — giant dragons that fly around the Land of Ice and Winter?' Emily and the others nodded eagerly; they had studied them in class.

'Well, a little while ago, one landed on a mountain,' said Madame Letsworth. 'His fiery breath is melting all the snow around him. He is causing avalanches and the rivers are turning from ice to water. If the dragon does not move soon, the land will be in grave danger of flooding and the towns near the foot of the mountain will be at risk of being destroyed by avalanches. We have to make him move or many sylphs and animals could die.'

'We were right then!' Molly whispered. She, Hannah and Emily had suspected that the Ice Princess might have something to do with a fire dragon.

'Fire dragons are stubborn creatures,'

Madame Letsworth continued. 'Once they have settled in one place, it is very hard to get them to move. But there is something that a girl not from this land, a girl like one of you with certain special qualities, can do to help.'

Emily stared. How could one of them ever move a dragon?

'What is it?' asked Molly curiously.

Madame Letsworth shook her head. 'I am not going to tell you more right now because if you know, it might make it harder for us to choose the right person, but I promise you will find out everything a week on Sunday.'

'It . . . it sounds very dangerous,' said Heather in a small voice.

'You would think that!' snorted Camilla, Emily's least favourite girl at school.

Madame Letsworth ignored her. 'The Ice Princess will certainly need great courage to face the dragon,' she told Heather. 'But we will use our magic to make sure no danger comes to her. Now that is all I am going to say for the moment. You have an hour before supper.'

Madame Letsworth left the room and the noise level rose instantly. Emily turned to her two friends. 'So the Ice

Princess *does* have to face a dragon!'

'I wonder what exactly she will have to do,' breathed Hannah. 'I wish Madame Letsworth had told us!'

'It's so annoying! I want to know more about how they're going to choose one of us,' said Molly. 'But doesn't the competition sound brilliant?'

Emily nodded. 'We'll have to work out who does what in our team. I hope we win.'

'Well, I hope *we* do,' said Amanda, who had overheard their conversation.

Emily frowned. 'You said you didn't even want to be in the competition!'

'I know, but seeing as I have to, I want to win it,' Amanda told her. 'I wish it was just skating on the rink though. I think I'll go down there now.'

'Shall we go too?' Emily said to Hannah and Molly. She could feel her feet itching to get back on to the ice. They nodded and set off for the rink after Amanda. Heather came too.

The ice rink at school was one of Emily's favourite places in the Land of Ice and Winter. The glittering white surface was smoothed out regularly by the frost fairies, tiny creatures about two centimetres high, who helped look after the girls. Above the ice was a clear glass roof. In the day you could see the sun and at night the dark sky, dotted with bright sparkling stars. Now Emily could see a magnificent sunset through the roof, pink and golden streaks covering the pale sky.

They all put on their skates. In her

locker, Emily kept the special snow-
white and scarlet skates that she had won,
although she usually wore her old
practice boots when she was skating in
lessons or with everyone else. She was
really proud she had won the special
skates, but she didn't want anyone to
think she was showing off.

'Let's play tag,' said Molly after they
had all warmed up with some simple
stretches. 'I'll be It!'

They scattered as she counted very quickly to ten. 'Coming! Ready or not!'

She raced after them. Molly was the fastest skater in the school. Hannah and Amanda were fast too – all three of them were in the advanced skating group, whereas Emily and Heather were among some of the least experienced skaters. Within a few seconds, Molly had tagged Heather. Heather set off after the others, but she didn't like going very fast.

'Come on, Heather. You can go faster than that!' called Amanda as Heather missed them again and again. 'Honestly, I can see who's not going to be the skater on our relay team!'

Emily saw a look of hurt flash through Heather's eyes. 'I'll be It with you,' she volunteered quickly. 'Let's try and catch them together!'

Heather shot her a grateful smile. 'Thanks, Emily.'

The two of them managed to corner Hannah and tag her. She quickly caught Molly who whizzed after Amanda.

'You're not so fast yourself, Amanda!' Molly said as she zipped in front of her, making her stumble and pull up.

'Molly!' Amanda exclaimed.

'Whoops, sorry!' Molly said innocently, darting away after tagging her. Emily was sure she had done it on purpose. Molly and Amanda always clashed.

They broke apart to skate on their own. Molly whizzed across the ice and threw herself into a triple jump, spinning round three times. She stumbled on landing, but just about kept her feet, laughing and skating on as her arms windmilled round. Looking composed, Hannah jumped an elegant double axel while Amanda spun round, her body arched dramatically back.

Emily set off round the rink. She loved the feeling of the ice under her skates. Speeding up, she did a double loop and then glided on one leg, her arms thrown back. She could do so much more now than when she had first started at the school four weeks ago. She turned into a layback spin. As Emily whizzed round faster and faster, happiness surged through her. Nothing was quite as much fun as skating!

Chapter Three
A Winter Wonderland

The next morning, Emily was woken up by something brushing against her face. She lay there for a moment wondering what was going on and then her eyes snapped open. Four little frost fairies were tickling her cheeks with their tiny fingers.

She grinned. 'Thank you!' She'd asked the fairies to wake her up extra early. No

one ever needed an alarm clock at skating school!

Jumping up, she shook Hannah and Molly awake. 'Come on!' she said as the frost fairies started pulling at their duvets to help her. 'We said we'd go to the kennels and see if we could take the huskies for a drive before breakfast, remember?'

The other two got up, yawning. The evening before, they had decided that Molly would do the skating part of the race because she was definitely the fastest skater and that Hannah and Emily would have another go at husky driving and decide who did the driving and who did the skiing. They set off for the kennels.

Trakin was watching as six of the huskies gambolled around a fenced-in paddock, rolling in the snow with each other. 'Hello, you three. What brings you out here so early?'

'We were hoping we could take a sledge out before breakfast,' said Hannah. 'We wanted to practise a bit more.'

'Great!' said Trakin. 'You can take a sledge each.'

'Really?' said Emily. 'Thanks!'

Trakin called to Dina, one of the other ice sylphs, and together they helped the girls get three teams of huskies ready to go. 'Just take it steady,' Trakin said, his eyes resting on Molly in particular. 'No going too fast.'

'And be careful as you reach the end of the line of trees.' Dina pointed to where they had been practising the other day. 'Do you see where the trees stop? You should go round to the left towards the forest, but just be careful because the huskies will try and go in the other direction.' She pointed to a hill behind them. 'There's a wooded gorge down there. The huskies love going for walks

in it and chasing arctic rabbits. If you're not careful, they'll try and pull you that way.'

'And it would be very dangerous on a sledge,' added Trakin. 'The trees have very low branches. You would get swept off very quickly. Make sure you keep a strong hold on the left rein when you get to the end of the line of trees.'

'OK, we will,' promised Hannah and they got on to their sledges.

The huskies were eager to be off and barked loudly as they started to pull, but the girls, even Molly, all drove sensibly and kept to a slowish pace, making sure they were always in control. When they reached the end of the trees, the huskies tried to veer to the right as Trakin and Dina had said they would, but the girls

pulled them firmly to the left. The
huskies gave in. As they headed out
across the field towards the forest, Emily
called across to the others, 'Should we go
faster?'

'Yes!' they both shouted back. The girls
urged the huskies on and rainbow sparks
from the dogs' paws rose up around the
sledges.

Emily laughed in delight as the world
whizzed by. She wanted to go faster and
faster! But she managed to resist the

urge, steadying the huskies as they reached the forest. Hannah and Molly also slowed down, and the huskies stopped barking and began to make happy wuffling noises as they settled into a steady trot.

'Isn't this amazing?' said Hannah. The early-morning sun was rising in the sky, its rays slanting through the tree branches and making the snow on the ground glitter and shimmer.

'It's beautiful,' Emily agreed, watching a silver-furred squirrel dart up a tree.

'There's some snow foxes over there!' said Hannah, pointing to one side. Emily caught her breath as she saw a white vixen proudly watching her four fluffy cubs playing in the snow. They were so cute!

The girls drove the huskies on down
the path, but after a bit, Molly reined in
her dogs. 'I'm thirsty!' She jumped off
the sledge and walked over to a nearby
tree. Like all the others, it had long
icicles hanging from its branches. Molly
reached to break one off, but as she did
so, it gave a wriggle and dropped to the
ground at her feet!

'Arghhhhhhh!' Molly squealed as the
icicle turned into a snake and slithered
away at top speed through the snow. She
gaped. For once, she seemed almost lost
for words as she pointed after it. 'Did
you see . . . what was that . . . oh, my
goodness . . .'

Hannah looked equally shocked. 'That
icicle was alive!'

Emily giggled. 'Don't be silly! Of

course it wasn't. It was an icicle snake.'

'What?' Her friends turned to look at
her.

'I read about them in one of the books
Madame Longley lent me.' Emily loved
this magic land so much she had asked
Madame Longley, the teacher who
taught them all about it, if she could
borrow books about the creatures who
lived there. 'Icicle snakes disguise
themselves as icicles and hang on tree

branches until their prey comes along. Then they drop on it and eat it.'

'Are they poisonous?' Hannah asked anxiously.

Emily shook her head. 'They swallow small mice and spiders whole, but they're not poisonous.'

Molly was staring after the icicle snake. 'Just think what tricks you could play with one of them,' she murmured, her eyes gleaming.

Emily jumped off her sledge and checked the tree out. There were two more icicle snakes. If you looked hard, you could see their tiny silvery eyes at the end of their bodies. She snapped off a real icicle and handed it to Molly. 'Here you are. A proper icicle!'

She got back on her sledge. As she

picked up the reins, she looked over. Molly had gone back to the tree. 'Come on!' Emily exclaimed.

Molly turned swiftly round, grinning. 'OK,' she said. 'I'm ready.' And they were off again.

It was brilliant driving through the woods and Emily didn't want to stop, but eventually they had to take the huskies back to the kennels and go inside for breakfast and lessons.

Their first lesson that day was about the Land of Ice and Winter. Emily got there early. She wanted to read more in the textbooks about the creatures they had seen on their sledge ride that morning. She was flicking through one from the bookshelf when Madame

Longley came in. She was an older ice
sylph with grey hair. 'Hello, Emily.'

'Hi. I was just looking up some
creatures I saw in the forest this morning.
I hope that's OK.'

'Of course,' said the teacher. 'What did
you see?'

'Icicle snakes, an arctic squirrel and
snow foxes. This is such an amazing
place!'

Madame Longley smiled warmly at

her. 'I'm glad you like it. Everyone who lives here thinks it is amazing too.'

'I love it!' Emily enthused. She remembered what Madame Letsworth had said and her brow furrowed. 'I hope the dragon can be moved on.' It was awful to think of parts of the land being in danger.

'If we choose the right person to be the Ice Princess then hopefully he will be,' said Madame Longley. 'But we must pick the right girl. She needs to have certain special qualities if she is to move the dragon.'

'What qualities?' Emily asked. But just then, the others started to come in and their conversation broke off.

Emily sat down. She was so busy thinking about the Ice Princess and the dragon that at first she didn't notice the look of excitement on Molly's face.

'Prepare for a fun lesson!' she whispered as she sat down. Emily stared. Molly's eyes were sparkling. It was how she usually looked before she played a trick on someone.

The class began. That day, Madame Longley was teaching them about some of the birds that lived in the land. 'The largest is the ice owl,' she said, going to the board and pulling down a picture of three different types of ice owl. 'Who can name these three?' Several people, including Emily, put their hands up. Madame Longley called Amanda out to write the names of the different owls on the board.

As Amanda went to the front, Molly

swiftly reached over and slipped
something into her pencil case.

'What are you doing?' Hannah hissed
from behind her. But Molly just grinned.

Amanda returned to her desk and
Emily and Hannah watched with bated
breath as she sat back down.

'Amanda, can I borrow your rubber?'
Molly whispered.

Amanda nodded and opened her pencil
case. As she did so, she let out a piercing
shriek and jumped to her feet, knocking
her chair over. 'Help!' she squealed. 'A
snake!'

Chapter Four
Classroom Chaos!

'Amanda, whatever are you doing?'
demanded Madame Longley as Amanda
shrieked even more loudly and jumped
on her chair.

The icicle snake slithered down
Amanda's desk leg and on to the floor.
Most of the class squealed and jumped
on their chairs too.

Madame Longley quickly scooped the

snake up and it froze in her hand. 'An
icicle snake,' she said. 'Girls, be quiet!'
Her voice snapped through the air. 'It is
perfectly harmless unless you're a small
mouse. Now sit down at once.'

Rather sheepishly, everyone sat back
down on their chairs. Madame Longley
held up the snake. 'Who is responsible
for this?'

'It was Molly!' burst out Amanda. 'I
know it was!'

Emily groaned inwardly as Molly

glared at Amanda. Although Amanda was right, her telling would only annoy Molly and make her play more tricks.

Madame Longley looked sharply at Molly.

'OK. It was me,' Molly owned up.

'I see.' Madame Longley frowned. 'So you brought the snake into class?'

Molly nodded. 'I'm sorry, Madame.'

'Well, seeing as you have chosen to waste my time then I will waste yours,' said Madame Longley. 'For the next week, you will spend your free time tidying out my cupboard. You will sort everything out and clean it. Do you understand?'

'Yes, Madame Longley,' Molly said in a subdued voice.

Madame Longley huffed. 'Now will you please take this poor snake outside back to where it belongs, Molly, and then we can all get on with the lesson.'

'I can't believe that I have to tidy out Madame Longley's cupboard in my free time all this week,' exclaimed Molly after the lesson. 'It's not fair and it means I won't be able to practise as much for the competition!'

'You did ask for it,' said Hannah. 'Bringing the snake into the lesson caused chaos.'

A grin caught at the corners of Molly's mouth. 'It was funny though, wasn't it? Didn't Amanda scream?' Emily and Hannah both giggled.

'She deserves another trick for telling

tales,' said Molly. 'I don't know why you're friends with her, Em.'

'She's not that bad,' Emily defended Amanda. 'I mean, I know she's bossy and she doesn't always think before she opens her mouth, but she can be nice too.'

Molly didn't look convinced so Emily changed the subject. She knew Molly would never agree with her.

'Right then, the competition. I guess the good thing is you're a really fast skater anyway, Molly, so you don't need to practise. But what about us? Which of us is going to ski and who will drive the huskies?' She turned to Hannah.

'You can do the husky bit if you want,' Hannah said. 'You were doing really well at it yesterday and I like skiing.'

'Brilliant! Thanks!' said Emily. 'I'll practise lots.'

'While I clean out cupboards,' sighed Molly.

After break, they had a skating lesson followed by free time. Molly went off to do her cleaning duty while Hannah headed to the ice rink and Emily went out to the kennels.

Dina helped her get the huskies ready. 'Have a good time!'

'Thanks!' Emily set off along the line of trees and then out towards the forest. The dogs bounded forward eagerly. Emily let them go faster and faster. As she reached the forest, she pulled back on the reins. For a few moments the huskies fought her, but then they slowed down.

'Good dogs,' she praised them as they entered the trees.

Ahead of her she saw Amanda, Heather and Olivia on their cross-country skis, practising for the race. Heather was lagging behind.

'Come *on*, Heather!' Amanda shouted at her in exasperation. 'You've got to go faster than that.'

'I'm trying,' said Heather, getting her skis in a muddle. 'I'm just not very good at this.'

'You're telling me!' Amanda muttered.

Heather fell over.

'Oh, honestly!' exclaimed Amanda.
'We're never going to win the relay race
if you can't ski better than this. You're
too slow to do the skating and not strong
enough to race the huskies. You *have* to
be able to ski!'

Emily reached them as Olivia pulled
Heather to her feet. 'Hi there.'

'Hi,' said Olivia and Amanda. Heather

didn't say anything; she looked close to tears.

'Are you practising for the competition?' Amanda asked Emily.

Emily nodded. 'I'm doing the husky driving on our team.'

'I'm going to skate of course,' said Amanda. 'I'm easily the fastest. Olivia wants to drive the huskies and Heather's going to ski – though she needs to get a lot better at it.'

'Don't worry, you'll get faster if you practise,' Emily said, smiling at Heather.

'And if she stops falling over,' sighed Amanda.

'Well, good luck,' Emily said. 'See you later! Come on, boys. *Mush!*' And flicking the reins on the huskies' backs, she let them bound away up the path.

Chapter Five
Helping Out

By the time Emily got back, her arms
were aching from controlling the huskies,
but she felt as if she was sparkling all
over. Heather was in the common room
and she didn't look very happy.

'How did the rest of the skiing go?'
Emily asked.

'Awful,' Heather admitted. 'I fell over
loads. Amanda says that if we lose, it'll be

all my fault. She keeps snapping at me for being useless and bossing me around.'

'Just ignore her,' Emily advised. 'I was her partner in the second week and she was like that with me too.'

'But you're not useless,' said Heather.

'No and neither are you,' Emily said.

'But I can't ski!' Heather protested.

'You managed fine when we did the scavenger hunt,' Emily reminded her.

'I guess,' admitted Heather. 'But at the moment I just keep falling over. I don't know what's wrong with me.'

Emily privately thought it was probably because Amanda was shouting so much. 'Look, why don't we go out skiing later? Maybe if I give you a bit of help, you'll soon be skiing really well again.'

'You'd really do that for me?' Heather said, hope lighting up her eyes.

'Of course,' said Emily cheerfully. 'I'll meet you at four o'clock.'

'Oh, wow!' Heather looked much happier. 'Thanks, Emily!'

At four o'clock Emily and Heather met by the back door with their skis. Emily had never been cross-country skiing until she started at ice-skating school. She found it quite difficult and tiring, but she

had got very good at it in the last few weeks.

The two girls pushed their boots into their skis and set off across the gardens, pushing the skis backwards as they moved. 'You want to try and keep your weight forward more,' Emily told Heather as she stumbled. Heather nodded and adjusted what she was doing.

'That's it,' Emily encouraged.

Heather went very slowly, but Emily didn't try and force her to ski faster. She just started to chat, hoping it would help Heather relax. 'Ballet was good this afternoon, wasn't it?'

'Yes, I really liked doing the free dance,' Heather replied. 'And the character work, but I couldn't do the attitude thing.'

'It's not that hard. You just have to keep your knee high and not wobble on your supporting leg,' said Emily. They chatted on about the ballet class as they headed towards the trees. Gradually Heather stopped stumbling and, without seeming to realize it, she started going faster and faster. Soon she was skiing in a really good rhythm with no wobbles at all.

When they reached the forest, Emily smiled. 'See, you *can* ski!'

'Oh, wow, I really can – oops!' Heather promptly fell over. 'See? I can't!'

'When you're not thinking about it, you're good,' said Emily, pulling her up. 'Maybe it's like skating. If you think too hard about what you're doing, it often makes you worse rather than better.

Come on, let's go a bit further and talk about lots of other things so you don't think about it!'

They skated on, talking about Charlie, the baby ice dragon who Emily and the rest of her dorm had been helping to look after the week before. He had now been put in with the older ice dragons who worked the music boxes in the school.

They soon reached a small hill. 'Come on! Race you down!' said Emily.

They charged their way down to the bottom and stopped in a dead heat. 'OK, now tell me you're not good at skiing!' Emily laughed.

Heather grinned. 'OK, you're right. I can do it. Thanks for making me realize that.'

Emily smiled back at her and they skied happily back to school.

Chapter Six
An Exciting Discovery

The next morning, Emily, Hannah and Molly went out into the woods to practise each of their skills for the competition. Not too far into the trees there was a long stretch of snow beside a frozen river. They all separated and then Molly shouted: 'Ready, steady . . . GO!'

Emily then leant forward. '*Mush!*'

The huskies raced across the snow to

where Hannah was waiting, her arm out. As they got closer, Emily started pulling on the reins. The huskies began to slow and, by the time she reached Hannah, Emily had the reins in one hand and the baton in the other, stretched out and ready. Emily thrust the baton into Hannah's hand and Hannah set off as fast as she could go to where Molly was waiting impatiently on the frozen river. Molly grabbed the baton from Hannah and started to skate, crouching low and using her arms as if she was an ice-hockey player. She whizzed up the river and shot past the tree they had marked as the end point.

'Yay!' Hannah cheered.

Molly turned round and skated back to where Hannah was, and Emily drove the

huskies to meet them. 'That was so cool!'

'And it's only our first proper practice,'
panted Molly, out of breath from skating
so fast. 'We'll be able to get even faster
than that by the competition!'

Just then, they heard the sound of
voices and saw Amanda and Heather.
Amanda was skating on the river and
Heather was skiing alongside. Heather's
practice session with Emily looked like it
had paid off and she was skiing better
than she had done the day before, but

she was still clearly not good enough for Amanda.

Amanda gave her instruction after instruction: 'Lean forward more . . . push harder . . . use your poles more . . . you've got to keep your chin up . . .'

The more Amanda said, the worse Heather got. She lost her rhythm and started to stumble.

'Oh, for goodness' sake, Heather! Can't you try harder than that?' scolded Amanda as Heather almost fell.

'Sorry,' Heather said quickly, blushing and looking to see if Emily, Hannah and Molly had heard. 'I'll try again.' But she was clearly flustered now and fell over a few moments later.

'Aargh!' exclaimed Amanda.

'Look, I'm . . . I'm not feeling well,'

Heather said. 'I'm going to go in.' She got up, her face burning, and skied away, falling over again in the process.

Emily jumped off the sledge and ran after her. 'Heather!' She helped her up from the snow. 'What's wrong?'

The other girl's eyes were full of tears. 'I'm so rubbish, Emily.'

'Don't start thinking like that again,' Emily said firmly. 'You *can* ski. You did yesterday.'

'But Amanda says I keep getting everything wrong.'

'Don't listen to her,' Emily insisted.

'Why? She's right. I am rubbish!' Heather pulled off her skis and, grabbing them in her arms, hurried away through the snow.

Emily's heart sank. She went back to

where Amanda was waiting on the ice.

'Heather's really upset.'

Amanda frowned. 'She just doesn't try.'

'Maybe you could encourage her
more, say nice things?' Emily suggested.

Amanda tossed her hair back. 'Or
maybe she should just pull herself
together,' she said tartly and, with that,
she turned and skated off.

★

Over the next few days, Emily tried to
help Heather, but it was hard. Whenever
she took her out skiing, Heather started
to improve, but it seemed to take only
one practice session with Amanda to
make her go to pieces again. No matter
how much encouragement Emily gave
her, she soon didn't even want to go out
with Emily either. Heather went around
at school looking increasingly worried.
Emily really wished there was something
more she could do.

In the meantime, Emily practised hard
with her own team. The days flew by.
From the moment the girls got up in the
morning to the time they went to bed,
every second seemed to be filled. If they
weren't skating or learning about the

land, they were practising or talking about the competition. All of the teams started timing themselves. Emily could feel her excitement growing. Who was going to win?

On the day before the competition, she and Hannah were on their way to supper when Molly rushed up to them, looking very excited. 'Look at what I just found while I was tidying Madame Longley's cupboard!' she said, waving a piece of paper at them. 'It fell out of one of the folders!'

Emily took it. There was a painting of a giant red dragon curled around a mountain. At the bottom of the mountain was a lake, and a girl in a white costume and silver skates was skating on it.

'Oh, my goodness! Is that the Ice

Princess?' said Hannah, looking over Emily's shoulder.

Molly nodded. 'Look at the writing underneath.'

Emily read it out: '*Legend tells that when a fire dragon lands on a mountainside and threatens all those about him, only the Ice Princess will be able to wear the silver skates and enchant him through the Lulling Dance so that he will fly away. She must be pure of heart, selfless and . . .*'

The words stopped.

'Where's the next page?' Emily asked eagerly.

'I couldn't find it,' said Molly. 'I've been looking for the last half hour.'

'Well, at least we know a bit more,' said Emily, reading the words again. 'So, the Ice Princess is going to have silver skates and she has to dance for the dragon.'

'But how does that get him to move?' said Hannah. 'And what's the Lulling Dance?'

They looked at each other, mystified.

'I guess we'll find out next week,' said Emily. 'It's cool to know a bit more though.'

Molly grinned. 'Yeah. At least cleaning out the cupboard hasn't been a complete waste of time!' She took the paper. 'I'd better put this back – in the correct alphabetical order of course. See you in the hall.'

Hannah and Emily continued down the corridor, talking about the Ice Princess. When they got to the hall, Emily spotted Heather getting a drink. She looked paler and more anxious than ever. 'Are you OK?' Emily asked, going over. Heather shrugged.

Emily saw the unhappiness in her eyes. 'Did you go skiing today?'

'Yes, and I was just as rubbish as always. I dropped the baton every time I gave it to Amanda and I fell over about ten times. Amanda's really cross with me. She says we're going to lose and it's all my fault.' Heather swallowed. 'It would be better if I wasn't in the competition. Amanda could do both the skiing and skating then. She and Olivia would be loads better off without me.'

'That's not true,' Emily told her.

Heather snorted and then rubbed her forehead miserably. 'Oh, I don't feel like eating. I'm . . . I'm going to my room.'

'Heather . . .' Emily began, but Heather was already hurrying away.

Emily went to join Hannah who had sat down with Tilda and Alice, the other two girls who shared the Frost Fairies dorm. 'Where's Heather gone?' asked Tilda in surprise.

'Back to her dorm,' said Emily. 'She said she didn't want any supper.'

'She's going to be so glad when this competition's over,' said Hannah.

'She looks really worried at the moment,' agreed Alice.

Emily sighed. She wished there was something more she could do to help.

They all got early nights, but Emily didn't sleep well. She had bad dreams and woke as the sun was just rising in the sky. She lay there for a few moments. She didn't have to get up for another couple of hours – it was so early that not even the frost fairies were up yet – but she couldn't get back to sleep. She kept thinking about Heather.

I wonder if she's awake? Maybe we could go out and practise a bit and I could cheer her up before the competition. Yes, that might work!

Getting out of bed, Emily pulled her clothes on. Then she went quietly down to the Ice Owls dorm. Olivia, Amanda, Tasha and Zoe were fast asleep, but Heather's bed was empty. Emily frowned. Where was she? Maybe she'd gone out practising already? Emily glanced out of the window and saw a small figure walking across the gardens towards the kennels. It was Heather! But she didn't have her skis. What was she doing?

Emily left the dorm and hurried after her.

Chapter Seven
Disaster!

By the time Emily reached the back
door, Heather had gone into the kennels.
Emily wondered what was going on.
None of the ice sylphs would be there
this early. Emily laced up her boots and
grabbed her skis and poles from the
locker. It would be quicker to ski across
the grass than walk. She set off across the
snowy gardens. It was a chilly, misty

morning, the sun hidden behind grey clouds.

Emily pushed herself across the snow, but as she got near to the kennels, she almost fell over in astonishment. A team of dogs were bounding away from the kennels with Heather driving them. She was urging them on, a determined look on her pale face.

'Heather!' Emily yelled. 'What are you doing?'

But Heather didn't hear her. She didn't look as if she could control the huskies very well. They fought her and ran on at whatever speed they wanted. They raced along the line of trees, barking excitedly.

Emily started skiing after them. She could tell they were starting to get out of control. To her alarm, she realized that

the dogs were veering round to the right
towards the gorge where the low trees
were. Emily's heart thudded as she saw
Heather pulling the left rein, trying to
change direction, but she wasn't very
strong and the dogs were in full gallop.
They ignored her and pulled round the
hill to the right.

'No!' gasped Emily as she saw Heather
starting to pull frantically on the reins
trying to stop them. The huskies ignored
her. Emily tried to ski faster, but she had

no chance of catching the dogs up.
Unless . . .

She looked at the hill to the right. The
dogs were racing round the base of it.
Maybe if she could climb up it, she could
then ski down the other side and cut
them off before they reached the woods.
Emily started hurrying up the hill. It was
difficult with skis and she was soon
gasping for breath, but she didn't stop.

At the top, Emily could just see the
huskies coming round the base of the
hill. Heather was still pulling on the
reins, her face terrified as they headed
towards the gorge. *If I can just ski down
the slope*, Emily thought, *then maybe, just
maybe, I can stop them before they get there.*

But could she do it? Skiing steeply
downhill on cross-country skis was really

hard because you couldn't turn to slow yourself down like you could with normal downhill skis. Emily took another look at Heather's terrified face. She didn't have a choice. *I have to try*, she thought. Taking a deep breath, she bent her knees and pushed off with her poles.

Within seconds, Emily's speed had built up and she was flying down the steep slope of the hill. She kept her knees bent low and her body crouched forward, her poles tucked through her arms and out behind her. The world hurtled by. She didn't think she'd ever skied so fast! Luckily the slope was covered with smooth snow and there were no obstacles in her way. She was going much too quickly to have been able to avoid anything. The speed whipped tears from her eyes, blurring her vision. As Emily neared the bottom of the slope, she saw the huskies approaching her.

Heather saw her at the same moment. 'Emily!' she screamed in horror.

For one awful moment, Emily thought she and the huskies were going to reach the same spot at the same time and crash into each other, but she reached the bottom of the hill just before they did. She skied straight into their path.

The ground levelled out and her speed slowed. Digging her poles into the snow, she kicked her skis round and slid to a stop, throwing up a cloud of snow crystals. Now there was no time to lose! Emily started skiing directly towards the huskies. 'Whoa!' she called to them, waving her arms. 'Whoa!' But the dogs kept going. They were almost on top of her!

Emily did the only thing she could: she crouched down and grabbed the harness as they charged past. She cried out as she was pulled along backwards on her skis, clutching the reins desperately, trying to stop the dogs and stay on her feet. 'Stop!' she cried. She had to halt them before they reached the low trees!

She felt the dogs starting to slow as her weight pulled them back. It felt like a lifetime, but within a few seconds, they had slowed from a wild gallop to a trot.

'Emily! You did it!' cried Heather.

She'd stopped them! Emily felt a massive sigh of relief escape her. She straightened up.

'Watch out!' Heather shrieked at the same moment.

Emily felt something bang into her head and then she knew no more . . .

'Emily! Wake up! Please! Wake up!'

Someone was shaking Emily's shoulder. Gradually she became aware of warm tongues licking her face and the feeling of cold underneath her. She was lying on her back. Her thoughts felt fuzzy and for

a moment she couldn't think where she was. Then suddenly she remembered – the huskies racing towards her, trying to stop them . . .

Her eyes blinked open and she saw Heather leaning over her. The huskies were all around her too. 'What . . . what happened?' she said, sitting up. 'Ow!' Her hand went straight to her head as a blast of pain shot through her.

'You hit your head,' Heather said, trying to pull the huskies off her. 'You stopped the huskies just as we got to the trees and tried to stand up, but there was a tree branch there and you hit your head on it. Then you just fell over. Oh, Emily, I thought you were dead!' She was almost in tears.

'I'm . . . I'm OK,' said Emily, although

she felt very strange. She looked up and saw the tree branches overhead.

Heather pulled the huskies away from under the trees and Emily crawled after her. 'What were you doing?' she asked Heather, trying not to think of the pain in her head. 'Why did you take the huskies out like that?'

Heather bit her lip. 'I was trying to run away.'

'Run away?' Emily stared.

'Not forever,' Heather said quickly. 'Just for today. I thought if I wasn't there then Amanda and Olivia could do the competition together and I wouldn't let them down. I knew I wouldn't get far enough skiing or skating and . . . well, I didn't want to be out all day on my own.' She stroked the huskies. 'So I thought I'd take a sledge. I was going to try and get to the Rainbow Pools and wait there until this afternoon then come back. I left a note for Madame Letsworth telling her I'd be back this evening.'

Emily stared at her. It was hard to take in. 'Oh, Heather.'

Heather looked really unhappy. 'The huskies got out of control and they galloped down here and I thought we were going to crash into the trees. But you stopped them, Emily. You were amazing!'

Emily's head was swimming. She didn't feel amazing. 'I'm glad I did. You just can't run off like that. You really can't.'

'I guess not,' said Heather in a small voice.

'Come on, let's go back to school,' said Emily. But as she stood up, pain shot through her and the world seemed to turn upside down. She sank quickly to her knees.

'What's the matter?' Heather said in alarm.

'My head . . . I-I feel really dizzy,' stammered Emily.

'You do look very pale,' said Heather anxiously. 'I'd better go back and get help. I don't want to drive the huskies, but I could use your skis.'

'No, I'll be OK,' said Emily, knowing how worried Heather would be at the thought of skiing back on her own. She took a breath and tried to stand again. 'I . . . I just need a few minutes.' She almost fell over as she tried to stand.

'No,' said Heather, helping her to sit back down. 'You can't ski back and you're not strong enough to take the huskies. You stay here and I'll go.'

Emily wanted to argue, but she felt too dizzy. Heather took her coat off and covered Emily's legs with it. She put on Emily's skis before freeing the huskies from the sledge. 'I'll be back as soon as I can,' she promised as the huskies crowded round Emily to keep her warm.

'Thanks,' Emily said shakily. 'Good luck. Will you be all right?'

'Yes, don't worry. I'll be fine,' said Heather. 'I can do this.'

Emily smiled. 'I know you can.'

Gritting her teeth, Heather set off.

Emily watched her go. At first, Heather stumbled a few times, but she didn't give up and soon she was speeding across the snow. Emily put an arm round the nearest husky's neck and leant against his reassuring warm body. She shut her eyes and waited . . .

Chapter Eight
Rescued

'Emily!'

Emily blinked. Madame Letsworth was skiing towards her. She was with Trakin and Dina, who were on a big sledge pulled by twelve huskies. Within minutes they had all reached her. 'Are you all right?' exclaimed Madame Letsworth. 'Heather told us what happened.'

'I'm OK,' said Emily. 'It's just my head. I banged it on a branch.'

'You must be concussed,' said Madame Letsworth. 'Let's get you back to school.'

Trakin lifted Emily up and put her gently on to the sledge, which was covered with thick fur blankets. 'I'll drive you home,' he said. 'Dina will bring the other dogs.'

'They've been keeping me warm,' said Emily as the dogs followed her to the sledge. She breathed out a sigh of relief. 'I'm glad Heather got back safely.'

'Silly girl,' said Madame Letsworth. 'She told me what had happened. I don't know what she was thinking of, trying to run away like that.'

'She was just a bit worried about the competition, but she's not silly,' Emily protested, her dizziness making her bold. 'She was brilliant. She was scared, but she skied back to get help for me. She was really brave.'

Madame Letsworth nodded. 'Yes, and she's not the only one, according to what she told me. She said you skied down the hill and stopped the huskies.'

'They were going to crash into the trees,' said Emily. 'I had to.'

'No, you didn't *have* to, you *chose* to,' Madame Letsworth said softly. 'You acted

very courageously, Emily. Well done.
Now let's get you back.'

Trakin got on to the sledge and, giving
Emily a cheerful grin, he started to drive
the huskies back towards the school.

Emily was taken to the sick bay where
Hannah and Molly were waiting anxiously.

'Goodness me, you three girls!' said
Matron, who had looked after Molly the
previous week after she had injured her
ankle. She shot a look at Hannah. 'It's not
going to be you next week, is it, Hannah?'

'I hope not,' said Hannah. 'Oh, Emily,
how are you feeling?'

'A bit sick still,' admitted Emily. 'But
I'll be OK.'

'Not well enough to go in the
competition though,' said Madame

Letsworth. Emily looked at her in dismay. 'No, absolutely not,' said the headteacher firmly. 'No skating or anything active for two days.'

Matron nodded to confirm this. 'It's important to rest with concussion, Emily.'

'You can watch the competition, but that is all,' said Madame Letsworth.

Emily felt awful. She looked at Hannah and Molly. 'I'm so sorry. I was stupid to bang my head. Oh . . .'

'Em! We're just glad you're all right,' said Hannah, taking her hand.

Molly nodded quickly. 'We were so worried when Heather came back and told us what had happened. The competition doesn't matter, Emily. It's you who are important.'

'We can do the competition with just

the two of us,' said Hannah. 'It would be loads better with you of course, but we'll be fine. Don't worry.'

'You'd better cheer us on though!' smiled Molly.

Emily felt relieved. She hated to let them down, but actually her head was really hurting and for once she didn't feel like husky driving. 'Thanks. Is Heather OK?'

'Yes, she is fine,' replied Madame Letsworth.

'Can I see her?' Emily asked.

'Yes, but then that is your last visitor. You need to rest so that you will be feeling well enough to watch the competition this afternoon. Hannah and Molly, you had better go and have breakfast now. Can you tell Heather she can come up?'

They nodded and set off.

Heather arrived five minutes later, looking really worried. 'Oh, Emily. I'm so sorry. I was so stupid to go off like that. If I hadn't then you wouldn't have got hurt and now you can't go into the competition . . .'

'It's all right,' interrupted Emily. 'Don't worry about it. I'll be OK, that's the main thing.' She smiled at Heather. 'You were brilliant. You skied all the way back on your own and got help. That was fantastic!'

'I thought I wasn't going to be able to do it,' Heather confessed. 'But I knew I had to because you needed me to and so I did. I thought about you all the way back and I didn't fall over once.'

'See! You can ski!' Emily told her. 'You are good at it. Maybe now you'll believe me!'

Heather gave her a shy smile. 'I think I will.'

'I bet you'll ski brilliantly in the competition,' said Emily. 'Don't let Amanda put you off before then.'

'Actually, since I got back, she's been really nice,' said Heather. 'I don't think she realized how upset I'd been about the practising. She was really shocked that I had tried to run away. She said she hadn't meant me to feel that bad; she'd just wanted to get me to try harder. It's made

me feel loads better. She's been really worried about you hurting yourself. She wanted to see you, but Madame Letsworth wouldn't let her come too.'

'Tell her I'll see her later,' said Emily. 'And good luck for the competition. I've got to support Molly and Hannah, but I'll be cheering you on too!'

Heather grinned. 'Thanks!'

'Come on now, Heather,' said Matron, bustling into the room. 'Time to give Emily some rest.'

Heather said goodbye. When she was on her own, Emily sank back against the pillows. Her head was aching, but she felt very happy. Thoughts of the competition flashed through her mind. What was going to happen? She might not be in it, but she couldn't wait to find out the result!

Chapter Nine
The Race

The competitors all lined up on the starting line in the forest. There were five husky sledges being driven by Molly, Olivia, Alice, Camilla and Clare. They had to race through the trees to where their partners were waiting on skis. The husky driver had to pass the baton and then the skier had to ski across a field to the river where the skaters were waiting.

Molly and Camilla, who were both doing two legs of their relay, would be driven by Trakin so that they would be waiting at the river when Hannah and Tess got there. Once the skaters had the baton from their teammates, they all had to skate back to school. The first to reach the stone steps at the front would be the winner!

Emily was watching from a sledge that Dina was driving. They would follow the huskies and the skiers and then stop to watch the skaters race home. It was very exciting. The teams of dogs were pulling at their harnesses. It was clear they were eager to be off.

Monsieur Carvallio, one of the skating teachers, was going to blow the starting whistle. 'Good luck!' Emily shouted to Molly.

'On your marks . . .' called Monsieur
Carvallio. The huskies all jostled into
position. 'Get set . . . GO!'

The teams set off, racing through the
woods, weaving in and out of the trees,
the huskies barking in excitement as
clouds of rainbow-coloured sparks flew
up in the air. Alice was doing really well
and was in the lead, closely followed by
Olivia. Both Molly and Camilla made
their dogs go so fast that they had trouble

turning them round the trees and they fell behind.

'Go on, Molly!' shouted Emily desperately. Molly got control of the dogs again and sent them racing after Alice and Olivia. By the time they came out of the trees, she was in third place.

She passed the baton perfectly to Hannah who set off on her skis. Olivia had made a perfect handover too, but Emily watched, heart in mouth, as Heather seemed to stumble.

'You can do it, Heather!' she shrieked from the sledge.

Gritting her teeth, Heather started to ski. To Emily's relief, she found her rhythm and was soon racing across the snow. She overtook Tilda and then gained on Hannah. Her eyes were fixed on Amanda who was waiting on the ice, urging her on.

Emily watched, torn in two as Heather caught up with Hannah. 'Go, Hannah! Go, Heather!' she shrieked as they both approached the river. Everyone was shouting now!

Molly and Camilla had jumped down from Trakin's sledge, changed into their skates and were now on to the ice.

'Well done, Heather!' Amanda cried. 'Come on. You're nearly here.'

And Heather was! She was the first to the ice. She passed the baton safely to Amanda, and Amanda took off, her face determined, her long dark hair flying out behind her. Molly grabbed the baton and chased after her. Camilla was close on her heels. Zoe and Helena, the other two skaters, were nowhere near as fast as the three leaders and they quickly dropped back, battling it out for fourth and fifth place.

Emily bounced up and down on the sledge, her headache completely forgotten. Molly had almost caught up with Amanda, but Camilla had almost caught up with her! They skated like ice-hockey players along the river. Who was going to win? The other girls in each team charged to the finishing line, all shouting and urging the skaters on.

Molly's going to do it! Emily thought in delight.

But just as Molly drew level with Amanda, Amanda found a final burst of speed and surged forwards. She swept across the finish line. Her team had won!

Emily felt a rush of disappointment for
Hannah and Molly, but when she looked
at them, she saw them hugging each
other, their eyes shining. They were so
caught up in the fun of it all that they
didn't look upset at all! They saw her
watching and Hannah came racing over,
leaving Molly to change out of her skates.

'Wasn't that an amazing race?'

'It was brilliant!' said Emily as Hannah
hugged her too. 'You did so well to
come second.'

'We'd have won if you'd been in the team, but it was so much fun anyway!' Hannah said.

'It's brilliant that Heather, Amanda and Olivia won,' said Emily, looking over to where the three winners were holding hands and jumping up and down.

'I'm really pleased for them,' said Hannah. 'Doesn't Heather look happy?'

Emily nodded. She'd never seen Heather look so ecstatic.

Madame Letsworth picked up a megaphone. 'Well done, everyone! That was a hard-fought and very exciting race. Will you all please come over to the school steps and we will have the presentation of the sky-blue skates.'

Everyone made their way over. Emily felt very grand being pulled along in

Dina's sledge! Madame Letsworth walked up the steps to a table. A cloud of frost fairies were fluttering above it.

'You have all done extremely well this week,' Madame Letsworth said. 'The other teachers and I were very keen to see how you would respond to the challenge and how you would get on working in your teams. The competitions are important in helping us decide who will be the Ice Princess. As you know, the girl who is chosen needs to have certain special qualities. Many of you have demonstrated these qualities in the last five weeks; the question is which one of you will make the best Ice Princess? Next week, our final competition will be a skating competition on the rink for a pair of silver skates. The Ice Princess will be announced after that. But now for the results of today's competition . . .'

The frost fairies formed a big number three in the air. 'In third place, Camilla and Tess. Well done, girls! It was a great team effort!'

Everyone clapped and Emily was surprised to see Camilla, who didn't usually take losing very well, actually smiling for once.

'In second place, Molly and Hannah, who did particularly well seeing as they hadn't practised as a pair until this morning.'

Molly and Hannah grinned at each other.

'And our winners are . . .' Madame Letsworth paused, 'Amanda, Olivia and Heather! Would you please come up to get your sky-blue skates, girls?'

The three girls ran up the steps and Madame Letsworth presented them each with a pair of blue skates.

'Congratulations,' she said warmly. 'You all did very well. In particular, Amanda, you skated superbly at the end.'

'Thank you,' Amanda said happily. 'But we wouldn't have won if Heather and Olivia hadn't been so good on their bits.

They were both brilliant!' She smiled at them.

Heather half put up her hand.

'Yes, Heather?' Madame Letsworth said.

Heather blushed shyly as everyone looked at her, but she took a deep breath and forced herself to speak out. 'I'd like to say a really big thank you to Emily. She's helped me so much this week with my skiing. She made me believe in myself and made me realize I could do it and . . . well, as everyone knows, she also rescued me this morning.' Her eyes met Emily's. 'I might have been the one injured if she hadn't saved me. Thank you so much, Emily. I wish you hadn't had to miss the competition.' Her face was bright red and Emily knew just how much it had taken out of her to speak up like that in front of everyone.

Around her, everyone cheered.

Thank you, Emily mouthed at Heather and the blonde girl smiled. A warm glow rushed all the way from Emily's toes to her head. She might not have taken part in the competition, but she had had a brilliant time and next week they were going to find out who was going to be the Ice Princess. How exciting was that?

Emily smiled in delight as she looked round at all her happy, laughing friends. Ice-skating school really was the very best place to be!

Do you dream of becoming an Ice Princess?

Have you ever wanted to go to a REAL Skating School?

All readers of *Skating School* get FREE membership to the National Ice Skating Association's Skate UK programme!

Skate UK will help you to learn all the moves and basic skills you need to become a true Ice Princess! It's all about fun and continuous movement and is taught in groups, so why not share your love of *Skating School* with your friends and bring them too?

To get your free membership, go to
www.iceskating.org.uk/skatingschool
and enter the secret password: **Twirl**.

Skate UK is taught by licensed NISA coaches and can be assisted by trained Programme Assistants.

For full terms and conditions visit:
www.lindachapman.co.uk
www.iceskating.org.uk/skatingschool

Do you want to enter super competitions,
get sneak previews and download lots of
Skating School fun?

Get YOUR skates on
join the
Sparkle Club
today!
lindachapman.co.uk

Just enter this secret password:

Twirl

The Land of Ice and Winter is waiting for you ...

Design your own ice-skating dress!

The tiny frost fairies have been working overtime designing the beautiful dresses for the girls to wear in the Ice-skating Academy competitions.

Using this dress as a template, the fairies need you to draw the most magical ice-skating outfit you can think of. Every month one lucky winner will receive a magical *Skating School* goody bag!

Send your drawing

with your name and address to:

Skating School Competition, Puffin Marketing, 80 Strand, London WC2R 0RL

Or e-mail them to: **skatingschool@uk.penguingroup.com**

Welcome back to the magical Land of Ice and Winter
... a world where all your dreams come true!

A brand-new *Skating School* series

Coming soon!

Hi there,

I hope you've enjoyed reading about the adventures of the girls who go to the Magic Ice-skating Academy. I love writing them all down! Wouldn't it be amazing to go to the Land of Ice and Winter and see all the creatures who live there? Can you imagine holding an actual ice dragon or talking to a frost fairy?

Sometimes readers write to me and ask about my life. Being a writer is the best job ever. I live in a cottage in a village with my family and two dogs – a Bernese mountain dog and a golden retriever. I spend my days writing and going to visit schools and libraries to talk about writing.

I always think I'm really lucky because I get to spend my days writing about magic – mermaids, unicorns, stardust spirits, genies and now the Land of Ice and Winter. If you love them too then why not go to **www.lindachapman.co.uk** and join the Sparkle Club? It's my online fan club with loads of activities and downloads, and you can only get to it by using the secret password at the back of this book. Have fun!

Love,

Linda
xxx

It all started with a Scarecrow

Puffin is well over sixty years old.
Sounds ancient, doesn't it? But Puffin has never been
so lively. We're always on the lookout for the next big
idea, which is how it began all those years ago.

Penguin Books was a big idea from the mind of
a man called Allen Lane, who in 1935 invented
the quality paperback and changed the world.
**And from great Penguins, great Puffins grew,
changing the face of children's books forever.**

The first four Puffin Picture Books were hatched in 1940 and the
first Puffin story book featured a man with broomstick arms called
Worzel Gummidge. In 1967 Kaye Webb, Puffin Editor, started the
Puffin Club, promising to **'make children into readers'**.
She kept that promise and over 200,000 children became
devoted Puffineers through their quarterly instalments of
Puffin Post, which is now back for a new generation.

Many years from now, we hope you'll look back and
remember Puffin with a smile. **No matter what your age
or what you're into, there's a Puffin for everyone.**
The possibilities are endless, but one thing is for sure:
whether it's a picture book or a paperback, a sticker book
or a hardback, **if it's got that little Puffin
on it – it's bound to be good.**